P9-DGE-465

For David and Gemma  –*GA*

To Rita Greene with much affection  –*VC*

**tiger tales**
an imprint of ME Media, LLC
202 Old Ridgefield Road
Wilton, CT 06897
Published in the United States 2002
Originally published in Great Britain 2002
by Orchard books, London
Text © 2002 Giles Andreae
Illustrations © 2002 Vanessa Cabban
Library of Congress Cataloging-in-Publication Data

Andreae, Giles, 1966–
  Heaven is having you / by Giles Andreae ; illustrated by Vanessa
Cabban.
      p. cm.
Summary: Grandma Bear believes that heaven is always around, especially
when Little Bear is there.
  ISBN 1-58925-016-8
  [1. Heaven—Fiction. 2. Love--Fiction. 3. Grandparents—Fiction. 4.
Bears—Fiction. 5. Stories in rhyme.]  I. Cabban, Vanessa, 1971– ill.
II. Title.
  PZ8.3.A54865 He 2002
  [E]—dc21

                        2001004570

Printed in Hong Kong/China

# Heaven Is Having You

by Giles Andreae

Illustrated by Vanessa Cabban

tiger tales

"It's heaven to see you!" said Grandma
As Little Bear rushed to her side.
"What's heaven?" asked Little Bear, hugging her tight.
"Let me see now…" his grandma replied.

It's not all that easy to tell you,
Because heaven is so many things.
Sometimes it's just seeing Grandpa Bear's face
As he's helping you play on the swings.

Sometimes it's something exciting

Like looking for monsters in dens.

But often it's just going walking together

Or watching you play with your friends.

It's feeding the ducks at the duck pond
And letting them eat from your hand.

It's seeing the wonderful shapes that you make
And the castles you build in the sand.

It's hearing the stories you tell us
And thinking that you're ever so clever.
It's something we do that we made up ourselves
Like rubbing our noses together.

It's chasing you around the garden

And hearing you shriek with delight.

It's lying down while you sit on my tummy

And tickle with all of your might.

It's having cookies with you for an afternoon snack
And getting some crumbs on our faces.
It's having our own little secrets to keep
And going to our own special places.

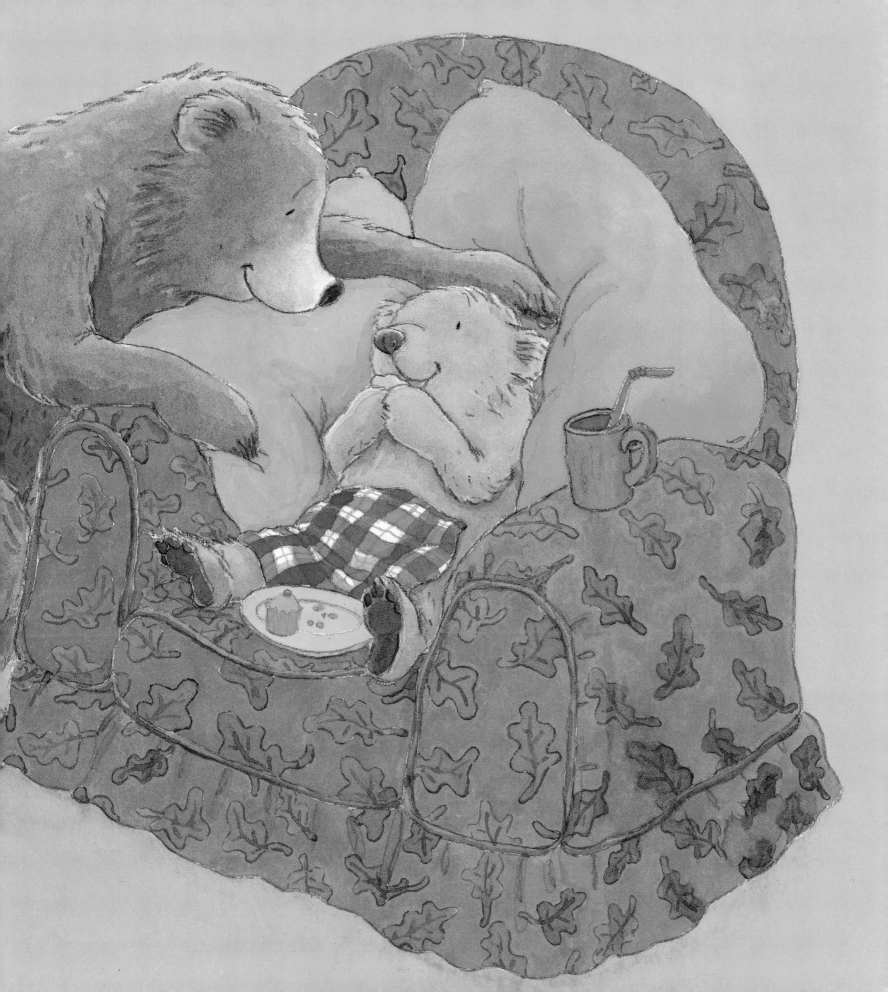

It's running a bath full of bubbles
And helping you climb right in.

It's holding you tight in a big fluffy towel

When it's my arms that you're in.

It's wrapping you up
    in a blanket
And feeling your warm rosy cheeks.

It's sitting and reading
a story together
And giving you special treats.

And then when it comes time for you to go home,
Heaven is kissing goodbye.

It's giving your grandpa
a big, lovely hug.
And it's seeing
the pride in his eye.

Heaven is always around us
In so many things that we do.

But one thing is true above all, Little Bear...

Heaven is just having you.